**START YOUR ENGINES!**

# KARTS

By Emma Huddleston

Kaleidoscope
Minneapolis, MN

## The Quest for Discovery Never Ends

...........................................................

This edition first published in 2020 by Kaleidoscope Publishing, Inc.

No part of this publication may be reproduced in whole or in part without written permission of the publisher.

For information regarding permission, write to
Kaleidoscope Publishing, Inc.
6012 Blue Circle Drive
Minnetonka, MN 55343

Library of Congress Control Number
2019940179

ISBN
978-1-64519-057-8 (library bound)
978-1-64494-215-4 (paperback)
978-164519-158-2 (ebook)

Text copyright © 2020 by Kaleidoscope Publishing, Inc. All-Star Sports, Bigfoot Books, and associated logos are trademarks and/or registered trademarks of Kaleidoscope Publishing, Inc.

Printed in the United States of America.

Bigfoot lurks within one of the images in this book. It's up to you to find him!

# TABLE OF CONTENTS

**Chapter 1: Fast and Light** ............................................. 4

**Chapter 2: Racing for Everyone** ................................. 10

**Chapter 3: Make Your Own** ....................................... 16

**Chapter 4: Competitions and Fun** ............................ 22

Beyond the Book ............................................................ 28
Research Ninja ............................................................... 29
Further Resources ......................................................... 30
Glossary .......................................................................... 31
Index ............................................................................... 32
Photo Credits ................................................................ 32
About the Author .......................................................... 32

# CHAPTER 1

## Fast and Light

Blake grips the wheel. Sharp turns pull him left and right. Kart sprint races are all about speed. This is a World Formula Light race. Blake faces fierce competition. He's fifteen years old. Most racers in this class are older than him. He doesn't mind. He likes the challenge.

Blake's kart has a new engine. Engines in this class are fast and powerful. Some reach speeds over 70 miles per hour (112 km/h).

### CLASSES OF COMPETITION

**Kart races are sorted into classes. They're grouped by age and engine type. Racers with similar skill and engine power compete. The "Kid Karts" class is for kids from five to seven years old. The karts have small 50cc engines. That's about the size of a chainsaw's engine. The Cadet class is for ages seven to twelve. The Junior class is for ages twelve to fifteen.**

In some racing classes, karts can reach speeds over 150 miles per hour (241 km/h).

Blake flies over the paved track. It's 0.75 miles (1.2 km) long. The kart is a few inches off the ground. Rods hold it together. The engine is behind the seat. Karts don't have a **body**. Blake passes karts with stylish body pieces. He keeps his kart simple.

Blake is happy to race in this class. At first, he did not think he would do well. But he finishes in third place! He celebrates with his family.

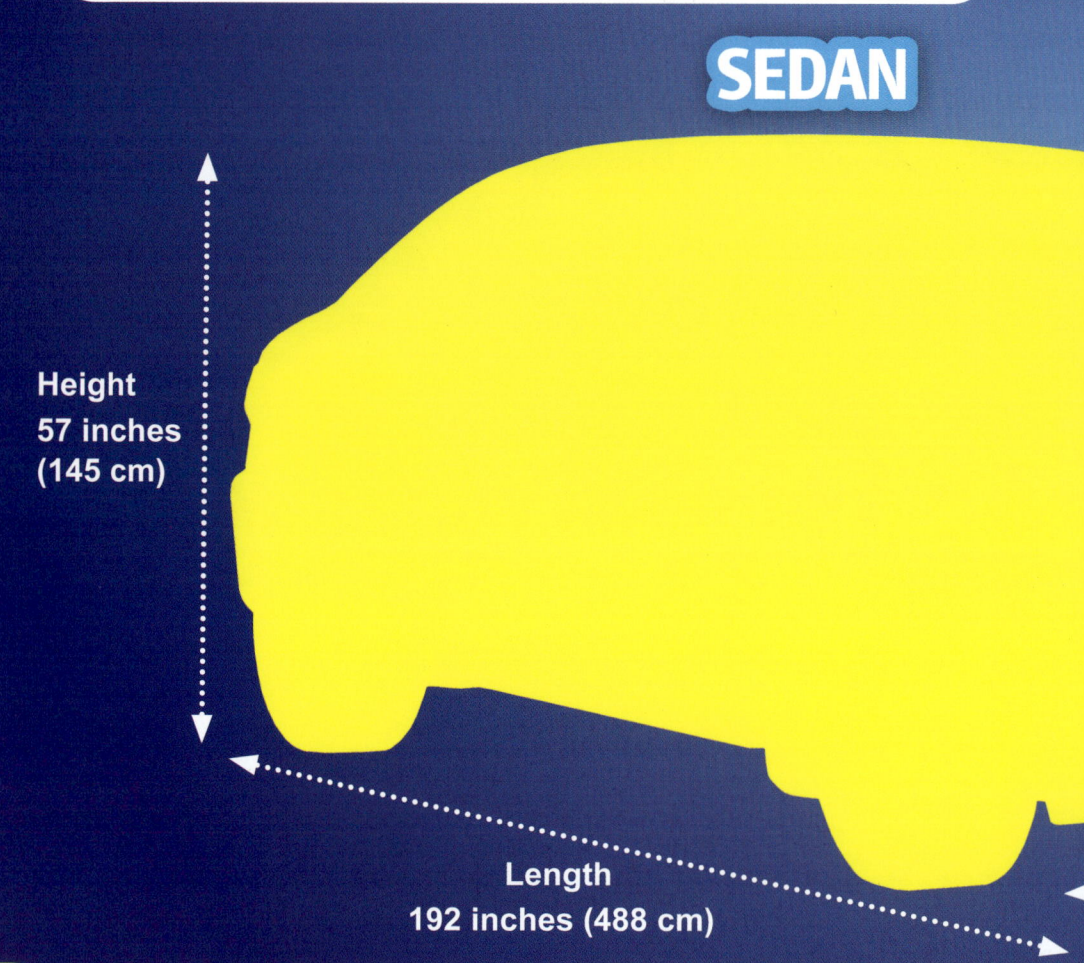

SEDAN

Height
57 inches
(145 cm)

Length
192 inches (488 cm)

# HOW BIG IS A KART?

## KART

**Height**
26 inches
(66 cm)

**Length**
72 inches (183 cm)

**Width**
50 inches (127 cm)

**Width**
72 inches (183 cm)

Hamda puts on her helmet. She climbs into her kart. It's time for practice. She chases her sister Amna's kart. Her wheels almost touch it. The sisters are from the United Arab Emirates (UAE). People call them the Emirati Speed Sisters. Hamda and Amna are making history. They show that racing isn't just for boys. They were the first professional female kart drivers in the UAE.

*More and more women are becoming involved in professional kart racing.*

**FUN FACT**
Amna and Hamda's father, Khaled Al Qubaisi, is a professional race car driver.

# CHAPTER 2

# Racing for Everyone

It was 1956. Art Ingels was a race car mechanic. His friend Lou Borelli worked on engines. They wanted to make a race car. But race cars were expensive. They wanted to make something everyone could use. They created the first kart. They used a lawn mower engine.

The first karts were made with inexpensive parts and didn't have bodies covering the frame.

The tires were made of thick rubber. The brake was simple. A lever pushed a metal disc onto the rear wheels. People refer to this kart as Kart No. 1.

Ingels rode his kart around his town. He drove in parking lots and tennis courts. The kart caught people's attention. They wanted to know where they could get one.

Three other men were inspired by Ingels's kart. They started the first kart company in 1957. They called the machines *go-karts*. The name stuck. The company sold kits to make karts. Each kit cost $129. Ingels and Borelli started a company, too. They sold a completed kart called the Caretta. Most people couldn't afford race cars. But many people could enjoy karting.

Kids and teens took up kart racing. They raced in parking lots. Paint stripes and rubber cones marked the tracks. Adults had races of their own. Soon, official groups formed in the United States. The groups organized races and made rules.

## MARIO KART COMES TO LIFE

*Mario Kart* is a popular video game series made by Nintendo. It inspires real-life kart races around the world. Racers dress up like the characters. The track looks like the game. There are even banana peel statues on the track.

*Early kart races took place in parking lots. Many karting organizations still hold races in parking lots today.*

Elwood Hampton was a machine worker in the 1960s. People called him Pappy. He built karts for fun. He used strong, light metals. He raced in a kart with a bright red seat. It carried him to many victories.

Pappy won the 1962 East Coast Championship. He was over fifty years old. Thousands of adults raced karts. But he was one of the oldest to race so well. That's how he got the nickname "Pappy."

More races were organized over time. Karting became popular around the world. **International** races still happen today. Karts have come a long way from Ingels and Borelli's Kart No. 1.

**FUN FACT**
The first Karting World Championship took place in Rome in 1964.

*Karting is an activity for racers of all ages.*

# CHAPTER 3

NASCAR star Jeff Gordon, along with many other professional race car drivers, got his start in kart racing.

## Make Your Own

Max looks up to Jeff Gordon. Gordon is a retired NASCAR star. He won ninety-three NASCAR Cup races. Gordon started out racing karts. Many professional racers did. Max wants to be a NASCAR driver one day. He asks his parents to help him build a kart.

Max paints the **chassis** blue. The chassis is important. The shape depends on the surface it will race on. Karts for paved tracks have a long front and narrow back. Karts for dirt tracks are the opposite. Max's kart has long bars on the sides. This makes it more flexible. It can handle sharp turns.

Max's dad looks for a motorcycle engine. But it's hard to find. They decide to use a lawn mower engine. It is still powerful. It has 5 **horsepower**. The kart will be able to go 40 mph (64 km/h). His dad connects the engine to the **axle**. He uses a chain. It looks like the one on Max's bike. But it's much bigger.

The kart takes a few weeks to build. Max's mom adds tires and a seatbelt. She tests the kart when it's finished. Max watches from the garage. Gas powers the engine. The kart rumbles when she starts it. A gear on the engine moves. The chain connects it to a gear on the rear axle. The engine powers both gears. They spin. The wheels screech. His mom rides down the driveway.

**FUN FACT**
Most standard kart engines run at 3,000 to 4,000 revolutions per minute (RPM).

A kart engine powers a chain that turns the axle.

# ZOOM IN ON A KART

Open seat
Engine
Steering wheel
Slick tires
Simple chassis
Front wheel axle

Next is Max's turn. He drives fast. His tires help him go even faster. Slick tires are best for paved surfaces. They don't have grooves. The tires make full contact with the ground. Max tries a tight turn. The chassis lifts slightly. The inside rear tire slides. He rides swiftly around the corner. He smiles. He can't wait to show his friends.

*Karts have slick tires, light chassis, and small, powerful engines to help them go faster.*

**CHAPTER 4**

# Competitions and Fun

Milo lives in Texas. He's at a racetrack with his family. His brother will race today. It's a **regional** karting competition. **Amateur** racers compete. Milo's brother wants to be a pro kart racer one day.

The oval track is 0.1 miles (0.2 km) long. It's made of soft dirt. Oval tracks are common in the south. People are familiar with them because of NASCAR. Milo spots his brother's kart. It's painted lime green and silver. The chassis is built for oval tracks. It can make tight left turns. The karts speed past. They kick up dust. Milo's brother crosses the finish line. Milo cheers. He came in first place!

### FUN FACT
Enduro kart races can last 30 minutes. Riders recline so they're almost lying on their backs!

Kart races may be held on sprint tracks, like the one pictured; oval tracks; or longer enduro courses.

Milo and his family walk around after the race. They get popcorn. Race day isn't just about competing. It's a community event. People can learn karting basics. Milo learns about different kinds of karts. He watches someone take apart an engine.

*In addition to races, many karting competitions offer activities and opportunities to learn more about karting.*

## KART STATS:
# DD2-CLASS KART

| ENGINE SIZE | NUMBER OF SPEEDS |
|---|---|
| 125cc | 2 |
| **BASE PRICE** | **HORSEPOWER** |
| Chassis $5,495, Engine $4,195 | 34 horsepower at 12,000 rpm |
| **TOP SPEED** | **SPECIAL FEATURES** |
| Approximately 80 miles per hour (130 km/h) | Silver, blue, and lime green chassis design details, extra soft seat, chainless drive system |

*Indoor karting tracks provide fun no matter what the weather is like outdoors.*

June is lucky to live in Connecticut. It has the largest indoor kart track in the world. SuperCharged Racing has two tracks. Some days, the two tracks are joined. They form one big SuperTrack. It is a 0.5 mile (0.8 km) track. One lap takes about two minutes. That's four times longer than a regular track.

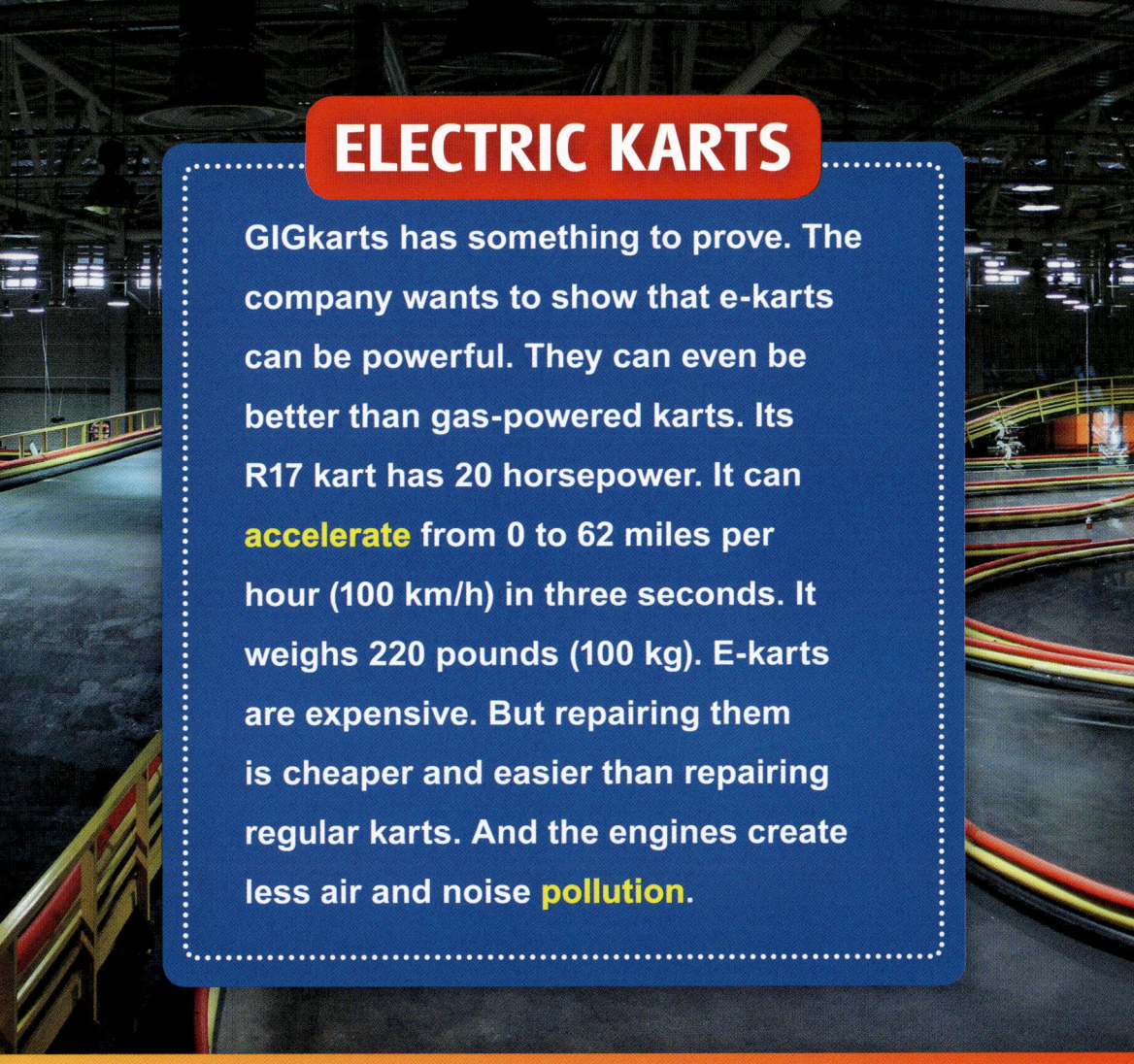

# ELECTRIC KARTS

GIGkarts has something to prove. The company wants to show that e-karts can be powerful. They can even be better than gas-powered karts. Its R17 kart has 20 horsepower. It can **accelerate** from 0 to 62 miles per hour (100 km/h) in three seconds. It weighs 220 pounds (100 kg). E-karts are expensive. But repairing them is cheaper and easier than repairing regular karts. And the engines create less air and noise **pollution**.

June grabs a helmet. She rents a kart. All of the karts are electric. E-karts are safer to use indoors. They run on batteries. The engines are quiet. And they don't create fumes. The air stays clean. Vroom! Her kart accelerates quickly. She drives around twists and turns. June likes driving around the track just for fun. Races are exciting. But people don't have to compete to enjoy karting.

# BEYOND THE BOOK

After reading the book, it's time to think about what you learned. Try the following exercises to jumpstart your ideas.

## THINK

**THAT'S NEWS TO ME.** *Mario Kart* kart races happen all over the world. Consider how news sources might be able to fill in more details about those events. What new information could be found in news articles? Where could you go to find those news sources?

## CREATE

**PRIMARY SOURCES.** Primary sources are documents that provide first-hand accounts of an event. Some examples include photographs, videos, and journal entries. Create a list of the kinds of primary sources you might be able to find about karts.

## SHARE

**WHAT'S YOUR OPINION?** June thought that e-karts were better than gas-powered karts. Do you agree with that opinion? Provide evidence to support your argument. Then, share your position and evidence with a friend. Does your friend find your argument and evidence convincing?

## GROW

**DRAWING CONNECTIONS.** Create a diagram that shows the connections between karts and NASCAR. How does learning more about NASCAR help you to better understand karts?

# RESEARCH NINJA

Visit www.ninjaresearcher.com/0578 to learn how to take your research skills and book report writing to the next level!

## RESEARCH

**DIGITAL LITERACY TOOLS**

### SEARCH LIKE A PRO
Learn about how to use search engines to find useful websites.

### FACT OR FAKE?
Discover how you can tell a trusted website from an untrustworthy resource.

### TEXT DETECTIVE
Explore how to zero in on the information you need most.

### SHOW YOUR WORK
Research responsibly—learn how to cite sources.

## WRITE

### GET TO THE POINT
Learn how to express your main ideas.

### PLAN OF ATTACK
Learn prewriting exercises and create an outline.

**DOWNLOADABLE REPORT FORMS**

# Further Resources

## BOOKS

Adamson, Thomas K. *Karts*. Bellwether Media, 2019.

Barger, Jeff. *Go-Karts*. Rourke Educational Media, 2016.

Mason, Paul. *Kart Racer: Lando Norris vs. Callum Ilott*. Franklin Watts, 2016.

## WEBSITES

Factsurfer.com gives you a safe, fun way to find more information.

1. Go to www.factsurfer.com.
2. Enter "Karts" into the search box and click 🔍.
3. Select your book cover to see a list of related websites.

# Glossary

**accelerate:** To accelerate is to go faster and faster. June presses the gas pedal in her kart to accelerate.

**amateur:** An amateur is someone who is not paid for competing, especially an athlete. Milo's brother is an amateur but hopes to be a professional one day.

**axle:** An axle is a rod that wheels are attached to. The axle spun the wheels and the kart began to move.

**body:** The body of a vehicle is its outer casing. To keep his kart light, Pappy didn't put a body over the chassis.

**chassis:** The chassis is the frame of a vehicle. A kart chassis is bare instead of being covered by extra metal and a body.

**horsepower:** Horsepower is a unit of power that measures how much work something is doing. Most karts have 5–10 horsepower, but some pickup trucks have over 300 horsepower.

**international:** Something is international if it occurs in or between more than one country. After Ingels introduced his kart, national and international organizations started holding races.

**pollution:** Pollution is waste in the environment that is unhealthy for people, animals, and plants. E-karts create less air pollution because the engines don't create fumes.

**regional:** A group of cities or states near each other makes up a regional area. Kart races have different levels of competition, including local, regional, national, and international.

# Index

axles, 18, 20

body, 6
Borelli, Lou, 10, 12, 14

Caretta, 12
chassis, 17, 20, 21, 22, 25

East Coast Championship, 14
engines, 4, 6, 10, 18, 20, 24, 25, 27

gas, 18, 27
Gordon, Jeff, 17

Hampton, Elwood "Pappy," 14
helmets, 8, 27
horsepower, 18, 25, 27

Ingels, Art, 10–11, 12, 14

Kart No. 1, 11, 14

*Mario Kart*, 12

NASCAR, 17, 22

steering wheels, 4, 20
SuperCharged Racing, 26–27

Texas, 22
tires, 11, 18, 20, 21

World Formula Light, 4

## PHOTO CREDITS

The images in this book are reproduced through the courtesy of: A_Lesik/Shutterstock Images, front cover (kart), p. 5 (bottom); Dande_lion_studio/Shutterstock Images, front cover (background); Jaggat Rashidi/Shutterstock Images, pp. 3, 5 (top), 25; Yauhen_D/Shutterstock Images, pp. 6–7 (car); Roland Magnusson/Shutterstock Images, p. 7 (kart); microgen/iStockphoto, pp. 8–9; Lynn Wineland/The Enthusiast Network/Getty Images, pp. 10–11; enchanted_fairy/Shutterstock Images, p. 12; subin pumsom/Shutterstock Images, p. 13; BangkokFlame/Shutterstock Images, pp. 14–15; Action Sports Photography/Shutterstock Images, pp. 16–17; Fluky Fluky/Shutterstock Images, pp. 18–19; Neil Lockhart/Shutterstock Images, p. 20 (kart); navee sangvitoon/Shutterstock Images, p. 20 (tire); Alexey Lesik/Shutterstock Images, p. 21; AAresTT/Shutterstock Images, pp. 22–23; Tachefoto/Shutterstock Images, pp. 24, 30; 977_ReX_977/Shutterstock Images, pp. 26–27.

## ABOUT THE AUTHOR

Emma Huddleston enjoys reading and swing dancing. She lives in the Twin Cities with her husband.